The Mystery of the
Dolphin Detective

THREE COUSINS DETECTIVE CLUB®

#1 / The Mystery of the White Elephant
#2 / The Mystery of the Silent Nightingale
#3 / The Mystery of the Wrong Dog
#4 / The Mystery of the Dancing Angels
#5 / The Mystery of the Hobo's Message
#6 / The Mystery of the Magi's Treasure
#7 / The Mystery of the Haunted Lighthouse
#8 / The Mystery of the Dolphin Detective
#9 / The Mystery of the Eagle Feather
#10 / The Mystery of the Silly Goose
#11 / The Mystery of the Copycat Clown
#12 / The Mystery of the Honeybees' Secret
#13 / The Mystery of the Gingerbread House
#14 / The Mystery of the Zoo Camp
#15 / The Mystery of the Goldfish Pond
#16 / The Mystery of the Traveling Button
#17 / The Mystery of the Birthday Party
#18 / The Mystery of the Lost Island
#19 / The Mystery of the Wedding Cake
#20 / The Mystery of the Sand Castle
#21 / The Mystery of the Sock Monkeys
#22 / The Mystery of the African Gray
#23 / The Mystery of the Butterfly Garden
#24 / The Mystery of the Book Fair
#25 / The Mystery of the Coon Cat
#26 / The Mystery of the Runaway Scarecrow
#27 / The Mystery of the Attic Lion
#28 / The Mystery of the Backdoor Bundle
#29 / The Mystery of the Painted Snake
#30 / The Mystery of the Golden Reindeer

YOUNG COUSINS MYSTERIES

#1 / The Birthday Present Mystery
#2 / The Sneaky Thief Mystery
#3 / The Giant Chicken Mystery
#4 / The Chalk Drawings Mystery

The Mystery of the Dolphin Detective

Elspeth Campbell Murphy

Illustrated by Joe Nordstrom

BETHANY HOUSE PUBLISHERS
MINNEAPOLIS, MINNESOTA 55438

The Mystery of the Dolphin Detective
Copyright © 1995
Elspeth Campbell Murphy

Cover and story illustrations by Joe Nordstrom

Three Cousins Detective Club® and TCDC® are registered
trademarks of Elspeth Campbell Murphy.

Published by Bethany House Publishers
A Ministry of Bethany Fellowship International
11400 Hampshire Avenue South
Minneapolis, Minnesota 55438
www.bethanyhouse.com

Printed in the United States of America by
Bethany Press International, Minneapolis, Minnesota 55438

Library of Congress Cataloging-in-Publication Data

Murphy, Elspeth Campbell.
    The mystery of the dolphin detective / Elspeth Campbell
Murphy.
       p.   cm. — (The Three Cousins Detective Club® ; 8)
    Summary: Ten-year-old cousins Titus, Timothy, and Sarah-Jane
go on vacation together and set out to discover why the dolphins
they are visiting don't seem to want to eat.

    [1. Mystery and detective stories. 2. Dolphins—Fiction.
3. Cousins—Fiction. 4. Conduct of life—Fiction.] I. Title.
II. Series: Murphy, Elspeth Campbell. Three Cousins Detective
Club® 8.
PZ7.M95316Myag   1995
[Fic]—dc20   95–45258
ISBN 1–55661–412–8   CIP
                                    AC

In loving memory of my father-in-law,
Howard R. Murphy,
whose life was filled with
love, joy, peace,
patience, kindness, goodness,
faithfulness, gentleness, and self-control.

ELSPETH CAMPBELL MURPHY has been a familiar name in Christian publishing for over fifteen years, with more than seventy-five books to her credit and sales reaching five million worldwide. She is the author of the best-selling series *David and I Talk to God* and *The Kids From Apple Street Church*, as well as the 1990 Gold Medallion winner *Do You See Me, God?* A graduate of Trinity College and Moody Bible Institute, Elspeth and her husband, Mike, make their home in Chicago, where she writes full time.

Contents

1. An Educational Vacation 9
2. Swimming With the Dolphins 12
3. Up, Up, and Away 17
4. Skip and Bubba 20
5. The T.C.D.C. 23
6. The Missing Watch 27
7. The Mysterious Light 30
8. Checking It Out 35
9. Disaster Strikes 39
10. Something Fishy 42
11. Dolphin Doctor 44
12. A Fish Out of Water 49
13. The Dolphin's Gift 52
14. Some Fish Story 56
15. The Gold Watch 58

1

An Educational Vacation

"*T*i, tell us again about this place where we're going," said his cousin Timothy Dawson.

"Wait a sec," said his other cousin Sarah-Jane Cooper. "I'm not ready yet."

She leaned back in her fancy carved chair and looked up.

When Timothy and Titus saw what she was doing, they leaned back in their chairs and looked up, too.

They were sitting in the lobby of Titus's apartment building with their suitcases beside them.

All around the top of the lobby, there was a mural painting right on the wall. The mural showed a deep blue ocean—with dolphins leaping and diving through the waves. In fact, the name of the apartment building was the Dolphin Towers.

Titus had studied that mural hundreds—no, *thousands* of times before. He had seen it every day of his life since he was a baby.

But he never got tired of looking at it.

Titus had always wished he could jump right into the picture and go swimming with the dolphins. He wished they could scoop him up and carry him laughing and splashing through the waves.

Then one day he found out there were some places by the ocean where that could really happen.

He found this out from his friend Professor Hartman. She lived in the Dolphin Towers and taught at the same university as Titus's father. Professor Hartman loved dolphins as much as Titus did. She had even written a picture book about them.

Timothy and Sarah-Jane knew Professor Hartman from visiting Titus. In fact, the three cousins, who had a detective club, had even solved a mystery for her.

So from the moment that Titus had found out that people could actually swim with dolphins, he started talking to his parents about it.

His parents called this pestering.

Titus called it polite reminding.

It just so happened that, earlier that year, Titus's parents and Timothy's parents and Sarah-Jane's parents had gotten together to plan their vacations. They had decided the cousins were old enough now—ten—to go on vacation with one another. And the parents had decided these trips should be Educational. With a capital E.

Well, Titus figured he could live with that. After all, what could be more educational than learning about dolphins? He just had to convince his parents.

But it turned out his parents were way ahead of him. (It was funny how often that happened, Titus thought.) His parents had already planned a trip to swim with the dolphins.

And now the time had come.

"OK," said Titus to his cousins in his best storytelling voice. "Let me tell you about this place where we're going."

Timothy and Sarah-Jane wriggled happily in their chairs. They had heard all this before, of course. But they wanted to hear it again.

2

Swimming With the Dolphins

Titus had never been to the place he was describing to his cousins. But he almost felt as if he had. His friend Professor Hartman had told him so much about it. She was working there this summer. And she had invited Professor and Mrs. McKay and the three cousins to come visit her.

"Anyway," Titus continued to Timothy and Sarah-Jane. "There's this bay right by the ocean where these scientists are working with some dolphins."

Timothy told the story along with Titus. "The scientists are teaching *tame* dolphins how to be *wild* dolphins."

"Exactly," said Titus. "The dolphins have already been trained for shows and movies and stuff like that. And they're used to people taking care of them."

Sarah-Jane said, "So, before they can go back to live wild in the ocean, they have to be *re*trained. They have to learn to take care of themselves."

"Right," said Titus. "But they still like to be with people. Even totally wild dolphins like to be with people. But the dolphins we're going to see are sort of tame and sort of wild all at the same time."

Now Titus was coming to his own favorite part of the story.

"There's this penned-off place right out in the bay where the dolphins live. And you can actually get into the water with the dolphins and swim with them. Except the dolphins don't have to come be with you if they don't want to. It's totally up to them."

"I hope they'll want to!" said Sarah-Jane.

"Me, too!" said Timothy.

"Me three!" said Titus.

They all laughed. But secretly Titus was a little worried. It was kind of scary, he thought,

13

to want something so much you couldn't stand
it.

He had worked very hard on his swimming
at the Y. You had to be a good swimmer to be
allowed in the water with the dolphins.

His parents had even gotten him a pair of
prescription goggles so that he could see well
underwater.

And now the Big Day was finally here.

Yesterday, he and his parents had taken his
little dog, Gubbio, to stay with Titus's grand-
parents.

This morning his cousins had arrived in the city.

And now the three of them were packed and waiting in the lobby.

As soon as his parents came down, they would all leave for the airport.

Titus felt as if he had been waiting his whole life for this trip. He couldn't wait another minute to get going. It was almost as if the longer he had to wait, the more chance there was that something could go wrong.

The elevator doors opened, and Titus's parents joined them.

"Well!" exclaimed Titus's father. "Ready for a trip to the ocean, boys and girls?" Except instead of "boys and girls," he said "buoys and gulls."

Everyone groaned.

Titus's father was always doing that—playing with words. Sometimes he liked to kid around by using words that sounded alike but didn't mean the same thing. It was called making puns, and it was very annoying. It drove Titus and his mother crazy. But people who make puns actually seem to like it when everyone groans.

See? Titus told himself. *Your father is making terrible puns. Everything is perfectly normal. You're just going on a nice Educational Vacation. So just calm down.*

What could possibly go wrong?

3

Up, Up, and Away

What could possibly go wrong? Well, nothing did. At first.

The airport and plane ride were uneventful.

Titus knew that "uneventful" didn't mean that *nothing* happened. It meant that nothing *unusual* happened. So a trip could be uneventful and exciting all at the same time.

The cousins had three seats right in a row. That meant they had to figure out how to share a window. Since takeoff and landing were the most exciting parts, they drew names out of Mrs. McKay's sun hat.

Timothy got the window for takeoff.

Sarah-Jane got it for landing.

And Titus got it for most of the time in between. Even that he was willing to share. His cousins were his guests. And besides, the really important part of the trip was yet to come.

The dolphins.

Tomorrow he would swim with them!

Or rather, he reminded himself, the dolphins would swim with him—if they wanted to. It was up to them. And Titus was OK with that.

He always felt that animals had the right to be exactly what they were. In Titus's opinion, there was no such thing as a yucky animal. A crocodile—in its own way—was every bit as wonderful as a Shetland pony.

Granted, you couldn't cuddle a crocodile. But whoever said you were supposed to? Not all animals were friendly to people. You had to use your common sense.

And if there was one thing people said about Titus it was: "That boy has a lot of common sense!" Teachers wrote that on his report cards. Neighbors said that to his parents when they asked if Titus could look after their pets while the owners were away.

Common sense told Titus that the dolphins might be skittish tomorrow. They might not come near.

But, oh, how he hoped they would!

Titus remembered a day in school when all the kids had to tell what kind of animals they would like to be. They were supposed to use their imaginations.

Titus had a lot of imagination along with his common sense. He had narrowed it down to a dolphin or an eagle.

He figured he would never know what it felt like to be an eagle. Eagles would never let you close enough to find out. Talk about un-cuddly animals!

But dolphins were another story altogether. They could be wild and free and up-close and friendly all at the same time. Dolphins actually let you *play* with them!

Titus was thinking all this as the plane landed and later when his parents rented a car. He was finally here. Tomorrow he would swim with the dolphins. A dream come true! He could hardly wait.

4

Skip and Bubba

*T*here were other places along the ocean where you could get close to the dolphins and even swim with them. But the place where the cousins were going was different. It was a small, quiet study center. Here the scientists could work with the dolphins away from the excitement of crowds.

Even so, dolphins who are used to people get pretty unhappy—even sick—if there are suddenly almost no people around.

So the center had a small guesthouse where a few visitors at a time could come and stay for a while. People who lived near the center could also stop by to visit.

But there weren't many kids in the area.

And the dolphins seemed to like kids most of all.

That's why Professor Hartman had been delighted to hear that the cousins were coming. She had said the dolphins would be delighted, too.

There were two dolphins at the center now. Their names were Skip and Bubba.

The study center was by the ocean on a quiet bay. Titus's parents had rented a car at the airport. And now they drove through a wooded area to the center, at the end of a winding road.

Professor Hartman came out to meet them. Titus was out of the car almost before it stopped moving. But as much as he liked Professor Hartman, she was *not* what he was dying to see.

Professor Hartman seemed to know this. She just laughed and pointed Titus toward the water.

Titus took off running with Timothy and Sarah-Jane right behind him.

They raced to the dock.

Then they stopped still and gasped.

Gliding toward them through the water

were two sleek, gray shapes.

Dolphins. Dolphins at last!

A dolphin named Skip.

And another named Bubba.

"EXcellent!" whispered Titus.

"Neat-O!" agreed Timothy softly.

"So cool!" murmured Sarah-Jane.

"Magnificent, aren't they?" said a voice beside them.

The cousins jumped.

It was getting on toward evening. And in the dusky light, they hadn't noticed anyone standing there.

5

The T.C.D.C.

*T*he person who went with the voice was an odd-looking woman—cozy and round, yet somehow mysterious, too. Titus thought she looked exactly like someone out of a fairy tale. Someone who would meet a traveler on the road and grant him three wishes or tell him what to say to a dragon.

Titus glanced at his cousins. They seemed surprised by the old lady, too.

"Ah, good evening, Mrs. Percival," said Professor Hartman, coming over with Titus's parents. "I would like you to meet my friends. This is Professor and Mrs. McKay, their son, Titus, and his cousins, Timothy and Sarah-Jane.

"Mrs. Percival is a neighbor of ours," explained Professor Hartman. "She comes over once in a while to visit the dolphins."

"They certainly seem to know you, Mrs. Percival," said Titus's mother. Indeed, the dolphins splashed back and forth as if trying to get the old woman's attention.

"Oh, no, my dear," said Mrs. Percival with a little laugh. "They're just curious is all. They don't see me often enough to know me. I'm afraid I don't get over here nearly as much as I'd like to. I can never even keep straight which one is which."

"The smaller, livelier one is Skip," explained Professor Hartman. "And the larger, cuddly-looking one is Bubba."

"Cuddly?" asked Titus. "Does Bubba really let you *cuddle* him?"

"He's been known to do that," said Professor Hartman with a smile. "He's been known to put his head right up on a person's shoulder when the person taps his shoulder. He's been known to let a person hug him—if it's someone he really likes and trusts."

Titus looked longingly at Bubba. But the dolphins seemed to have lost interest in the visitors for some reason and swam away.

Oh, well, thought Titus. *Maybe tomorrow.*

"Of course, we're gradually trying to get them to be less dependent on people," said Professor Hartman.

"Yes, how's that going?" asked Titus's father.

"Quite frankly, not as well as we had hoped," she replied. "Dolphins in captivity are usually fed herring that is flown in from the north. Our plan here was to attract local fish into the pen so that the dolphins could learn to catch their own food. We were making progress. But suddenly Skip and Bubba lost interest in learning to catch their own food. They don't even seem hungry when we offer them their regular meals. And yet they seem healthy, even happy."

"So what you're saying, Carolyn," said Titus's father, "is that these dolphins are as happy as *clams.*"

"Dad," muttered Titus. "You're doing it again."

Professor Hartman laughed. "You'll never cure him of that, Titus. But maybe you and Timothy and Sarah-Jane can solve the mystery of the happy dolphins for us. Maybe we need the T.C.D.C."

"What's a 'teesy-deesy'?" asked Mrs. Percival.

The cousins almost jumped again. They had almost forgotten she was there.

"It's letters," explained Sarah-Jane. "Capital T. Capital C. Capital D. Capital C. It stands for the Three Cousins Detective Club."

"Goodness! What time is it?" asked Mrs. Percival. "Silly of me. I never wear a watch."

"It's a little past six," said Mrs. McKay.

"Then I must go straight home and see about my dinner," said Mrs. Percival. "It's a longish walk up the road, you know. Goodbye, everyone. It was *so* nice to have met you! And good luck with your detecting!" she added to the cousins.

With that, she turned and scurried away. Scurried—that was the right word for it, Titus thought. Just like someone out of a fairy tale.

He wondered why such a nice old lady would lie about not wearing a watch.

6

The Missing Watch

"*H*ow do you know she was lying?" Timothy asked Titus later when the cousins had a few minutes alone.

"Because I saw the mark on her left wrist before she shoved her hands into her pockets," said Titus. "The rest of her arm was tan from the sun. But there was a band of lighter skin around her wrist. It was shaped like a watch."

To demonstrate, he took off his own watch and showed them the lighter skin underneath. Titus said, "If you *never* wore a watch, your arm would be tan all over."

"That still doesn't mean she was lying when she said she never wore a *watch*," Sarah-Jane pointed out. "I mean, maybe she wears a bracelet most of the time. Maybe the bracelet is sort of shaped like a watch, and maybe that's what left the mark."

"It's certainly possible, S-J . . ." said Titus slowly.

He had to keep reminding himself that a good detective has to keep an open mind. A good detective has to be careful not to jump to conclusions.

Sometimes, when you're good at figuring things out, you can get to thinking that whatever you figure out must be right.

But sometimes you can figure things out in a way that makes sense, when, in fact, that isn't the way things are at all.

Titus thought all this over. Then he shook his head. "I don't know. I *still* think Mrs. Percival wears a watch all the time—at least enough so her wrist didn't tan where the watch was. And for some reason the watch is missing. And for some reason she told us she never wears a watch. That's my theory, anyway."

"But why would she lie about a stupid little thing like that?" asked Timothy. "You shouldn't lie at all, of course. But usually people lie because they think they have to. To stay out of trouble or something like that."

Titus shrugged and said with a grin, "It's just my theory. I didn't say it had to make sense."

Sarah-Jane said, "If Mrs. Percival lied about wearing a watch, does that mean she lied about other things, too?"

They thought back to what Mrs. Percival had said. None of it had seemed all that important. Why would you lie about not getting over to see the dolphins very often?

Again, all Titus could do was shrug.

A good detective has to admit to himself when he doesn't have the slightest idea what is going on.

A good detective collects bits of information and files them away in the back of his mind in the hope that they will make sense later.

So that's just what Titus did when—late that night—he saw a mysterious light bobbing along where no light should be.

7

The Mysterious Light

*I*t was a standing joke among his relatives that Titus "went to sleep fast and woke up slow."

To say he was a sound sleeper was an understatement.

People were always saying, "That boy could sleep through a tornado. That boy could sleep through a hurricane."

But there were always exceptions to the rule. The night before Christmas was one. The night before he was going to swim with dolphins was another.

Professor Hartman had introduced Titus and his parents to the other workers at the center. After that, they had all gone out to dinner together. Then the visitors had come back to the guesthouse and settled in, tired out from traveling.

But Titus had trouble getting to sleep. Too much excitement maybe? The first night in a strange bed? Too many questions playing tag in his head?

He had tossed and turned for a while. Then, at last, he got to sleep. But when he woke up again, it was still dark, not yet dawn.

Titus went to the window and looked out.

In the city it never got completely dark, not with all the streetlights and traffic. That's why it was so hard to see stars in the city. The lights from the ground got between you and the sky.

In the country, the sight of all those stars took Titus's breath away.

But then he saw another light. This one was a few feet above the ground. And it bobbed along toward the study center. But it wasn't coming along the road—it was in the wrong place for the road.

What could it be?

As Titus was wondering about this, the light suddenly disappeared.

Titus stood for what seemed like a long time, staring at the spot where the light had

last been. Had he imagined the whole thing?

In the city it never got completely quiet. But when you listened in the country, you realized it was not completely quiet there, either.

Titus stood at the window, straining his eyes and ears. He heard the gentle lapping of the bay, and farther off, the muffled roar of the ocean itself.

Then he heard a rustling noise, like branches blowing in the wind. *That's funny,* Titus thought to himself. *I didn't think there was even that much of a breeze tonight.*

But wait!

Something had excited Skip and Bubba!

Titus could hear them splashing and chattering away in "Dolphin," their mysterious language of clicks and whistles.

After a little while, the dolphins settled down.

The sky began to lighten with the approaching dawn. If the bobbing light appeared again, Titus didn't see it. He had crawled back into bed and—in spite of all he had seen and heard—had instantly fallen asleep.

The next thing he knew, Timothy was shaking him.

He heard Timothy say, "Honestly, Uncle Richard! This son of yours could sleep through an earthquake!"

And his father was saying, "Are you kidding? That boy could probably even sleep through one of my classes! Wake up, Titus. Rise and shine. It's Dolphin Day."

That did it.

Titus came fully awake.

But after breakfast, he pulled his cousins aside to tell them what he had seen and heard in the middle of the night.

8

Checking It Out

*T*itus had to get them to stop laughing first. His cousins seemed to find the idea of him wide awake in the middle of the night hilarious.

"Ex-*cuse* me?" said Timothy. "*You* couldn't sleep? *You?*"

Sarah-Jane said, "You could sleep through a—"

"I know, I know," Titus broke in. "But this is important. So listen up."

The cousins had an unwritten rule that if one of them wanted to be serious, the others had to quit kidding around and listen.

So Timothy and Sarah-Jane stopped their teasing and listened to what Titus wanted to tell them.

But when Titus had finished telling them about the light and the excited dolphins, Timothy and Sarah-Jane just looked at him without saying anything.

"You *do* believe me, don't you?" asked Titus.

"I believe that *you* believe you saw it," said Timothy carefully.

"That's not the same thing!" protested Titus.

"I know it isn't," Timothy admitted. "But how do you know you weren't dreaming, Ti? It seems kind of unreal."

"What about you, S-J?" said Titus.

"You didn't believe me that time I saw a weird face in the lighthouse window," Sarah-Jane reminded him.

"I sort of believed you," said Titus.

"All right, then," said Sarah-Jane in her that-settles-it tone of voice. "It's all right for me to sort of believe you now."

And Titus was actually OK with that.

The cousins had another unwritten rule: They always had to listen to one another. But they didn't always have to agree.

And that led to another rule: When in doubt, check it out.

"What did that light look like again?" asked Timothy. "You said it was 'bobbing.' You mean like someone carrying a flashlight?"

"Yes!' cried Titus, realizing for the first time what it was he had seen. "Yes, that's exactly right. Someone carrying a flashlight."

"And *where* did you see it?" asked Sarah-Jane.

"Down near the water. Right over there."

All three of them looked in the direction Titus was pointing. They could see nothing but overgrown bushes.

But the rule was: When it doubt, check it out. So they went to take a closer look.

When they reached the bushes by the water, the dolphins made a beeline toward them.

Titus said, "They look like Gubbio when he knows I'm getting him a dog biscuit." It sounded like an odd thing to say, even to his own ears. But that's just what Skip and Bubba looked like.

Timothy started swatting at the bushes.

"Wait a minute!" said Titus. "That's the sound I heard last night. Like branches blowing in the wind. Only . . . there *was* no wind."

The cousins looked at one another. Without another word they pushed back the bushes. And that's how they found the hidden path.

9

Disaster Strikes

*I*t wasn't much of a path. But someone had taken the trouble to cut away the weeds and overgrown bushes.

There was a bend in the path that kept the cousins from being able to see where it led. But they knew better than to follow the path and go wandering in strange woods by themselves. There were some things you could check out. And there were some things you couldn't. You had to use your common sense.

Still, what they could see right in front of them was interesting enough.

The grass was worn down into parallel lines. The lines looked like marks a car would make. Except that they were *way* too small to have been made by a car.

What then?

The cousins looked at one another, silently asking themselves that question.

"A baby buggy?" suggested Sarah-Jane.

They all knew she didn't really think someone had been pushing a baby buggy through the woods. But sometimes saying the first thing that pops into your head is a good way to get your thinking started.

"A shopping cart?" joined in Timothy.

"No," said Titus suddenly. "A *wagon*!"

And somehow Sarah-Jane and Timothy knew that he was right. Though why anyone would be pulling a wagon through the woods in the middle of the night was beyond them.

They didn't have time to think about it, though, because just then Titus's father came to call them to change for swimming.

All Titus knew was that one second he was turning to go back to the house. And the next second, he was sprawled on the ground with horrific pain in his ankle.

10

Something Fishy

*T*imothy and Sarah-Jane plunged back through the bushes calling for help.

Titus's father practically flew over to them, with Titus's mother right behind.

"What's happened?" they asked. "Did you trip on something?"

"I didn't *trip*. I *slipped*," said Titus.

"On what?"

"I don't know."

His parents didn't think the injury was serious. Even so, they packed the ankle with ice and whisked Titus off to the emergency room for X-rays.

Fortunately, the ankle wasn't broken, just sprained. And fortunately, the sprain wasn't even that bad.

But it still hurt like crazy.

The doctor was very gentle as he wrapped the bandage around Titus's ankle.

But what he said was surprising.

"Something smells fishy about you, kid!"

"What?" asked Titus in alarm.

"Your shoe," replied the doctor. "It smells as though you stepped on a fish. Get it? Something fishy?"

Titus groaned, and not just from the pain in his ankle. How many people like his father *were* there in the world? And was he—Titus McKay—going to run into *all* of them?

The question of how he could have gotten a fishy-smelling shoe ran through his mind. But then he had to be fitted with crutches, and that took all of his attention.

Crutches aren't that easy to use. It takes a lot of upper-body strength to manage them. Fortunately, Titus had built up his upper-body strength with all his swimming practice at the Y.

Titus was feeling pretty good about that when reality hit him like a thunderbolt.

With a sprained ankle, he couldn't swim.

11

Dolphin Doctor

*T*imothy and Sarah-Jane had an announcement to make. Titus could tell the moment the car pulled up in front of the guesthouse.

His cousins stood solemnly side by side.

"What's up, kids?" their uncle asked them as he helped Titus to hobble out of the car.

"We talked things over," began Timothy.

"And we decided something," added Sarah-Jane. "We decided that if it turned out Ti's ankle was hurt so bad that he couldn't go swimming . . ."

Timothy finished the thought. "Then we wouldn't go in the water, either."

But Titus wouldn't hear of it.

He had had time to think all this through on the way home from the hospital.

Yes, this was probably the worst day of his life. But that didn't mean it had to be the worst day of *everyone's* life, did it?

He knew it would drive him crazy to see Timothy and Sarah-Jane in the water with the dolphins when he couldn't go in. But that wasn't their fault, was it?

Kids weren't allowed to go swimming without a grown-up. Mrs. McKay said that her husband should go in with Timothy and Sarah-Jane and that she would sit on the dock with Titus.

But Titus wouldn't hear of that, either. He knew both his parents were dying to swim with the dolphins.

His mother protested. Titus insisted.

So in the end his mother just got all weepy and hugged him hard. And his father said he was really growing up—the way he cared about other people's feelings.

While the others went to change, Titus slowly made his way down to the dock. It was weird feeling so grown-up and brave and downright *lousy* all at the same time.

It took some doing, but he managed to sit down and make himself almost comfortable.

45

He looked out over the water toward the dolphins. The longing to jump into the water and swim out to them was almost unbearable.

Then something absolutely amazing happened.

The dolphins stopped their playing, turned, and swam directly over to Titus. Their friendly, smiling faces popped out of the water, just inches from his injured ankle.

Titus was aware that Professor Hartman had come and sat down quietly beside him.

He turned to her. "How did you do that?" he asked. "How did you make them come over to me?"

But Professor Hartman just smiled and shook her head. "I didn't do anything," she said. "They probably came because they sensed you have an injury."

Titus stared at her. "Skip and Bubba know I sprained my ankle?"

"Not exactly. But dolphins seem to be able to sense when another dolphin is sick or injured. Then they'll gather round the one in trouble and lift it to the surface so it can breathe if it can't do that on its own.

"There are even stories about dolphins

saving people from drowning by carrying them to land. The dolphins seemed to know that people can't live in the water."

"Wow," said Titus softly. "Wow."

"So anyway," Professor Hartman continued, "scientists are wondering if getting some gentle attention from dolphins can actually help sick people to get well."

"*I* feel better. That's for sure," said Titus. "Can I touch them?"

"Yes," Professor Hartman replied. "Just don't pat them on the 'melon lump' on their foreheads. They don't like that. But otherwise they love to be petted."

Titus reached out and stroked the curious noses that were pointed at his ankle.

The dolphins felt kind of rubbery to the touch.

They felt kind of wonderful!

As Titus patted them, they chattered away at him.

Titus, who didn't speak a word of Dolphin, understood exactly what they were saying.

It was: "Oh, you poor kid! What happened to your ankle? Tell us all about it!"

Well, it was either that or: "Fish! We want fish!"

Titus wasn't really sure which.

The thought of fish stirred up other thoughts in the back of Titus's mind.

There was something he had to do.

If only he could remember what it was.

12

A Fish Out of Water

"You want us to do *what*?" asked Timothy.

He and Sarah-Jane had dried off after their swim and were eating a picnic lunch with Titus under a shady tree.

"I know it sounds crazy," Titus said. "But it's just something I have to check out. I have this theory about how all these mysterious things might fit together." He paused and sighed deeply. "But I can't get around very well because of these crutches."

Sarah-Jane rolled her eyes. "Oh, puh-leese!"

Titus laughed. He never would have thought he'd be laughing on the worst day of his life. But he owed it all to Bubba.

Timothy and Sarah-Jane had had a wonderful swim. Skip had played with them.

But Bubba had never left Titus's side. It was as if he had understood completely how hard it was on Titus not to be able to go into the water.

Bubba the dolphin reminded Titus a lot of Gubbio, his little dog.

On the surface of things, the dolphin and the Yorkshire terrier didn't look anything alike. But Titus was thinking about who they were inside. They both had the same kind of personality. Sweet and gentle. Just the nicest animals you'd ever hope to meet. They gave you lots of sympathy and cared about your feelings.

And this, thought Titus, was a pretty good way for anyone to be. It didn't matter if you were a dolphin or a dog or a person.

"So anyway," Titus said to his cousins, getting back to the subject at hand. (Or, as his father would say, at *foot*.) "The point is, when I fell, it wasn't because I *tripped*. It was because I *slipped*."

"And you think you slipped on a fish," said Timothy.

"Right," said Titus.

"In the woods," said Sarah-Jane.

"Right," said Titus. "Call me crazy, but—"

"You're crazy," said Timothy and Sarah-Jane together.

"Then humor me," said Titus. "All I know is that I slipped on something when we found the hidden path. And the doctor said my shoe smelled fishy. If I slipped on a fish, I'm thinking maybe it skidded under a bush or something. Just go look around the hidden path where we were standing. See what you can find. I'd go myself"—Titus paused again and sighed—"only I don't know how I could look through the bushes with these crutches. . . ."

"OK, OK," said Timothy.

"We're going. We're going," said Sarah-Jane.

13

The Dolphin's Gift

While his cousins went off to look for a fish on dry land, Titus hobbled back down to the dock and watched the dolphins playing.

Soon Bubba swam over to greet him.

"Hi! How're you doing, boy?" Titus asked him.

Bubba presented Titus with a little gift.

"Ooo! Seaweed!" said Titus, genuinely delighted. After all, it's the thought that counts. "You're the sweetest little dolphin in the whole world, aren't you?"

Bubba nodded happily.

Titus would have felt a little silly talking baby talk to such an enormous animal if he hadn't overheard one of the trainers doing the same thing the day before.

There was something Titus wanted to try. He was a little bit afraid to. But he knew he'd never forgive himself if he passed up the chance.

He got himself situated so that he wouldn't be knocked off balance. Then he leaned closer to the dolphin and patted his own shoulder.

Would it work?

Would it?

It did!

Bubba rose partway out of the water and placed his head gently on Titus's shoulder. Titus threw his arms around Bubba and cuddled him. As he did, Titus said to himself, "I will remember this moment for the rest of my life."

Then Skip came by with more seaweed, and the two dolphins swam off.

Titus was dripping wet from being hugged by a dolphin and having seaweed dropped on his shoe.

One thing was for sure: Between stepping on fish and having seaweed dumped on them, his sneakers would never be the same again. Maybe his mother would let him "retire" them. Maybe get them bronzed, like baby shoes.

He was just wondering about this when Timothy and Sarah-Jane came running back, breathless with excitement.

"Ti! Ti! You were right!" cried Timothy. "We *did* find a fish. Right about where you thought it might be."

"Or rather—" corrected Sarah-Jane. "We found what was left of the fish after you stepped on it. 'Yucky' doesn't quite cover it."

"But there was still enough of it left that we could tell what it looked like," said Timothy.

"And guess what!" exclaimed Sarah-Jane. "That fish is not from around here. We looked it up. Guess what kind of fish it was. Go ahead—guess."

Titus decided it was time to really put his theory to the test.

"A herring?" he asked.

"Bingo," said Timothy.

Skip and Bubba, perhaps sensing that something exciting was going on, came swimming over.

Bubba had brought another gift—more of the seaweed the nice boy seemed to like so much.

"Thank you, Bubba!" said Titus.

But then something caught his eye.

There was something tangled up in the seaweed. Something golden that glinted in the sun.

Carefully, the three detective cousins pulled away the soggy seaweed to see what else Bubba had brought them.

It was a watch with a broken clasp.

And on the back of the watch there was an inscription: *To A.P. from J.P. with all my love.*

"Well," said Titus after a long silence. "I think it's time we talked to some grown-ups."

14

Some Fish Story

*I*t took a while—quite a while—to explain what Titus's sprained ankle had to do with the dolphins not being hungry.

"Someone's been feeding them," explained Titus. "Someone has been loading up a wagon with herring and pulling it through the woods in the middle of the night. One of the fish fell off, and that's what I slipped on."

Timothy said, "The thing is, Skip and Bubba have been getting plenty of the kind of fish they're used to. And they don't even have to hunt for it."

And Sarah-Jane added, "That's why they're not interested anymore in learning to like a new kind of food. Let alone learning to catch it for themselves."

"Kids," said Professor McKay. "That sounds like some kind of fish story."

Titus groaned. He knew that a "fish story" was any unbelievable tale. The name came from fishermen who exaggerated about how big the fish were that they caught. Or the ones that got away.

"Dad!" pleaded Titus. "Please don't tell me it smells fishy. The doctor already said that about my shoe."

"On the contrary," said his father. "I said it *sounds* like some kind of fish story. But I think what you're saying is true."

"So do I," said Professor Hartman with a worried frown. "But we can't release Skip and Bubba into the wild if they can't catch their own food. Feeding them on the sly will only keep them at the center. Who's doing this? And why?"

Sarah-Jane shook her head apologetically. "We just know who. We don't know why."

15

The Gold Watch

*W*hen she heard the cousins' explanation, Professor Hartman phoned Mrs. Percival and politely asked her to come over to the center for a talk.

"My goodness, what happened to your ankle?" Mrs. Percival immediately asked Titus.

"I sprained it when I slipped on a herring," Titus said.

There was a muffled gurgle from Timothy. And Titus realized how funny that sounded.

But Mrs. Percival had turned very pale. "Oh, no!" she said. "Oh, no! Oh, Titus! I'm *so* sorry!"

Titus handed her the watch. "This is yours, isn't it, Mrs. Percival?" he asked gently.

"It's exactly the size and shape of the untanned part of your wrist."

Mrs. Percival's eyes filled with tears. "Yes, the watch is mine. My late husband, Jim, gave it to me. I wear it all the time. But the clasp broke. And my heart just about broke when I lost it. But I couldn't say anything because I knew I'd lost it when—"

"When you were feeding the dolphins," said Sarah-Jane. "Bubba brought us the watch tangled up in a present of seaweed."

Mrs. Percival smiled. "That Bubba is a darling, isn't he? They both are. Skip is more mischievous. He'll play tricks on you. But Bubba is just a sweet old teddy bear."

"Then you *can* tell them apart," said Timothy.

Mrs. Percival went from turning pale to blushing. "What must you all think of me! I've done nothing but lie. I am a very foolish old woman."

"But why did you do it?" asked Sarah-Jane. "Why did you feed the dolphins?"

"Because I am also a very lonely old woman," said Mrs. Percival with a sad little smile. "When my husband died, I thought I would go crazy. But I got into the habit of coming here every morning at dawn. Not telling anyone, just coming in the back way and spending a little private time with the dolphins. And that actually gave me some strength to get through the day. I really believe they somehow knew I was hurting.

"Of all God's creatures, dolphins are my favorites. So beautiful. So graceful. So gentle.

"But then I recently found out that the scientists weren't just studying Skip and Bubba. They were training them to leave. And I thought I couldn't bear to see them go."

Titus nodded. He could understand that.

Mrs. Percival looked at him gratefully. Then she continued her story. "So I thought . . . I thought maybe I could slow down their progress a little. I never meant any harm—though I knew what I was doing was wrong.

"I'm actually glad you found out." She gave an embarrassed little laugh. "It was getting expensive to have the herring flown in. I had to pretend to be a fish market. Oh, dear! What must you think of me?"

She turned to Professor Hartman and said earnestly, "I want you to know that I fed them only the finest herring. I inspected the fish thoroughly."

"I'm sure you did," said Professor Hartman. "And I'm sure I have your word that this won't happen again."

"Oh, absolutely!" said Mrs. Percival.

"Then I can't see any harm's been done," said Professor Hartman. "Come visit the dolphins whenever you want to. When the time comes for them to leave, they'll let us know. And we'll know it's the right thing for them."

Mrs. Percival nodded. She looked very peaceful.

Titus said, "Maybe Bubba will let you cuddle him before it's time to leave."

Everyone looked at him in astonishment as he told the wonderful, wonderful, wonderful story of how he got to hug a dolphin.

Later, Titus and his parents and his cousins walked down to the dock and watched Skip and Bubba leaping and diving through the gentle waves of the bay.

Professor McKay said, "When you sprained your ankle, Titus, I almost couldn't bear it. I knew how disappointed you must be.

But the day hasn't turned out too badly, has it?"

"No," said Titus, keeping a straight face. "It's been very Educational."

There was something else he had been saving up to say to his father. And this seemed as good a time as any.

"Dad?"

"Yes, son?"

"It wasn't an accident when Bubba brought us that watch."

"It wasn't?"

"No," said Titus, trying *very* hard to keep a straight face. "He did it on porpoise."

The End

Series for Young Readers*
From Bethany House Publishers

THE ADVENTURES OF CALLIE ANN
by Shannon Mason Leppard
Readers will giggle their way through the true-to-life escapades of Callie Ann Davies and her many North Carolina friends.

ASTROKIDS™
by Robert Elmer
Space scooters? Floating robots? Jupiter ice cream? Blast into the future for out-of-this-world, zero-gravity fun with the AstroKids on space station *CLEO-7*.

BACKPACK MYSTERIES
by Mary Carpenter Reid
This excitement-filled mystery series follows the mishaps and adventures of Steff and Paulie Larson as they strive to help often-eccentric relatives crack their toughest cases.

THE CUL-DE-SAC KIDS
by Beverly Lewis
Each story in this lighthearted series features the hilarious antics and predicaments of nine endearing boys and girls who live on Blossom Hill Lane.

JANETTE OKE'S ANIMAL FRIENDS
by Janette Oke
Endearing creatures from the farm, forest, and zoo discover their place in God's world through various struggles, mishaps, and adventures.

THREE COUSINS DETECTIVE CLUB®
by Elspeth Campbell Murphy
Famous detective cousins Timothy, Titus, and Sarah-Jane learn compelling Scripture-based truths while finding—and solving—intriguing mysteries.

*(ages 7–10)